ORCHARD BOOKS

First published in Great Britain in 2022 by Hodder & Stoughton

1 3 4 7 9 10 8 6 4 2

A CIP catalogue record for this book
is available from the British Library.

ISBN 978 1 40836 569 4

Printed and bound in Great Britain by Clays Ltd, Elcograf S.p.A.

The paper and board used in this book are made from
wood from responsible sources.

Orchard Books
An imprint of
Hachette Children's Group
Part of Hodder and Stoughton
Carmelite House
50 Victoria Embankment
London EC4Y 0DZ

An Hachette UK Company
www.hachette.co.uk
www.hachettechildrens.co.uk

XTINCT!

T-REX TERROR

ASH STONE

Special thanks to
Shari Last

CONTENTS

1

Jeevan's BMX soared across the forest floor. Barrelling past thick branches that scraped against his helmet, he swerved in and out of deep shadows, throwing up dirt, a smile spreading across his determined face. He pedalled hard, whipping through grasping leaves, sharp like claws, until – *nooo!* He turned and braked at the last moment, trying to do a

CHAPTER ONE

180 spin, but lost his balance. Luckily, he
managed to stop himself from skidding
down a surprisingly steep drop.

*Better not break any bones before
dinner*, he thought with a grin.

Jeevan unclipped his helmet and sipped
from his water bottle. He was out of
breath. Even his old skate park hadn't
been this exciting, this . . . dangerous.
Not that he was going to admit as much
to Mum.

Squawk!

Jeevan ducked as a black feathered
creature swooped just in front of him.
For a wild moment, he thought it was an

T-REX TERROR

Archaeopteryx, but that would be crazy.
It was just a crow. All of Mum's talk about
fossils was making him think about ancient
creatures.

Jeevan always felt like he had to play
down his dinosaur obsession around his
friends back home – he wasn't sure it
was cool to be dino-mad at his age. But
out here, miles away from his friends,
Jeevan's love for dinosaurs didn't need to
be hidden. Plus, as much as he was angry
about the whole moving-to-a-new-home
thing, he couldn't *help* but get drawn in
when Mum talked about fossils.

The crow dived to the ground. It flew

so close to him – probably because it had never seen a human before. This whole forest had an undisturbed wildness to it. Jeevan looked up to the tops of the huge oaks and pine trees. Everything had a glimmering, greenish hue.

Standing still, Jeevan could make out more and more movement around him. Butterflies fluttered, squirrels skittered and birds twittered. Rustling bushes told him there were larger creatures about too. He spotted some spiky branches poking out from behind a blackberry bush. They looked like Triceratops horns. Far in the distance, tall, thin trees were swaying, just like the long necks of Brachiosauruses. And what was that sneaking across the forest floor? A club-tailed Ankylosaurus . . . ?

Nope. It was a hedgehog. Not quite an Ankylosaurus, but still, being this close to a hedgehog was pretty unusual. He'd never seen one back in the city. It disappeared under a large bush. Jeevan didn't mind – he wasn't here for the local wildlife. He was on the hunt for something a bit less *current*.

Last time he'd walked through the forest, it was with Mum, who was telling him about the fossils she was going to be working on in her new job. Even though she was talking about fossils, Jeevan barely listened;

he was still so angry that she'd made him move from the city to here, the middle of nowhere.

". . . and that's why, if we analyse the DNA of ancient animals, maybe we could save some endangered species today," Mum had said, while Jeevan walked grumpily beside her wheelchair. "Who knows," she'd continued, "we might even be able to re-introduce extinct species."

Blah, blah, blah, Jeevan had thought, scowling as he stepped in something brown and suspiciously squishy. *Who cares about endangered species? What about me? I'm endangered now. As far as my friends are concerned, I'm about to go extinct.*

But that was weeks ago, and Jeevan was a lot less angry now. True, he still had no idea what his mum did in her lab all day – he didn't understand what she was talking about half the time – but he couldn't pretend he didn't love fossils.

So this afternoon he'd decided to go exploring to find more of them. All the fossils at the lab had been found in a bog at the edge of the forest, but Jeevan couldn't remember which way it was. He'd seen the bog when flying his drone above the lab; it stretched out at the foot of the large hill. He

CHAPTER ONE

wished he had his drone now, but Mum had confiscated it when he flew it inside her fancy lab.

Another noise startled Jeevan. He heard some twigs snap ahead. Just past the treeline, in a small, overgrown clearing, he saw movement. Something big. And could he hear voices?

Jeevan picked his way down the incline, wheeling his bike along. Slowly, he approached the clearing and leaned his bike against a tree. There was nothing there, just a thick layer of bushes, bracken and long grass. Rolling his eyes at the fact that he'd been expecting some sort of creature to come stomping through the forest, Jeevan walked a bit further and was happily surprised when his foot slid into soft, squelchy mud. The bog.

Jeevan wasted no time. He grabbed a stick and started digging. Mum had enough fossils of her own in that weird, fancy lab. She let him look but never touch. Now he was going to find the best fossil of all.

The mud was gloopy and thick, making it hard to dig. But Jeevan kept at it. Then, with a *thunk*, his stick hit something solid.

Scrabbling with his fingers, Jeevan pulled out something hard, about the size of his thumb. It felt smooth and had a shallow depression at one end. It *could* be a fossil. Maybe some ancient wolf or bear fell into the bog thousands of years ago. Or maybe . . . just maybe . . . could it be a bone from the spine of a Velociraptor? Or a Stegosaurus tail vertebra? *Why not?*

Just then, Jeevan heard the sound again. Twigs snapping under the feet of something heavy. Something big. It was coming from back where he'd left his bike. He crouched and looked up past the bushes. His heart was hammering again, and he sensed the creature before he saw it. A shadow emerged from the trees, bigger than he'd expected. It was a deer.

Jeevan almost laughed, but stopped himself. He didn't want to scare it away. What did he think it was going to be anyway? A T-Rex?

The deer was so close he could see the green of its eyes and the white flecks in its shiny brown fur. It stepped gracefully into the clearing, lowering its head to graze. Jeevan was reaching for his phone to take a photo when he heard another noise, this time through the trees to his right – voices.

He saw two figures move just behind the treeline. One tall, one short, and both carrying long sticks.

"It's just what he's looking for," said the taller figure, a woman. "Plenty of wildlife. Nice and remote." Her companion muttered something, but Jeevan couldn't make it out.

"Mr Fox will be pleased with me— I mean, us," the woman continued.

She stepped into the clearing and her eyes widened. She touched her finger to her lips, motioning for her companion to keep quiet. She'd spotted the deer.

The second person, a man, stepped out from the trees and Jeevan's breath caught in his throat: the woman had raised the stick she was holding. But it wasn't a stick; it was a rifle.

In the single moment it took for the woman to assume a hunting stance,

Jeevan's mind flew
over what was
about to happen.

Just as her finger
tightened on the
trigger, Jeevan
sprang up from his
hiding place and
shouted, "GO!
Run!"

The deer darted
back into the forest just as a sharp gunshot
rang out through the trees.

Jeevan watched the spot where the deer
had disappeared, relieved at the animal's

escape, before glancing back at the hunters. The woman stood stock still, the man at her side. Then she turned slowly towards Jeevan until the rifle was pointing directly at him.

2

Acting on pure instinct, Jeevan ducked and rolled to his left. He clambered, climbed and crawled out of the bog and through a thick tangle of bushes.

Which way? He couldn't get his bearings; his mind was in a blind panic. He forgot all about his bike and just ran. His legs moved with a mind of their own, carrying his body through the forest.

T-REX TERROR

Jeevan ran and ran but eventually had to stop. He was completely out of breath.

He listened carefully. No voices, no snapping twigs. No ringing gunshots. Just his own heavy breathing. He looked around, relieved to discover he was near his mum's lab at the edge of the forest. Maybe his legs had known where they were going, after all.

He jogged past the last of the trees and came out on to the path that wound between the lab and his house. He'd made it.

The lab was a boxy, ultra-modern building totally at odds with the wild

CHAPTER TWO

trees that surrounded it. Bursting through the doors, Jeevan's skin turned cold as the blast of air conditioning hit his clammy forehead. "Mum," he yelled into the echoing space. "Where are you?"

"In here, Jeevan," came his mum's quiet voice. Dr Anjali Kaur was in the main lab, an open-plan workspace with white walls and stainless-steel surfaces. She was staring into a microscope, as usual.

Jeevan darted up to her, still out of breath. "I was cycling through the forest, Mum, and then I saw this deer—"

"Oh, that's nice." Still peering into the microscope.

CHAPTER TWO

"Yes, but then I heard something else—"

"What was it darling? Let me guess . . . a—" She twiddled the dials on the microscope.

"No, Mum. Listen."

"Just because I'm looking into a microscope doesn't mean I'm not listening." One eye shut, squinting into the microscope with the other.

"I know, Mum. But—"

"I just need to finish this analysis before the specimen turns—"

"MUM," Jeevan interrupted loudly. "There were these *hunters*. They were going to shoot—"

His mum's head snapped up.
"Hunters?" Her expression clouded.
"*Hunters?*"

Jeevan nodded.

"Are you okay?" Before Jeevan could answer, his mum continued, "Hunters in *this* forest?"

"I—"

"I don't want you running around on your own if there are hunters about, Jeevan. Okay? Promise me?"

Jeevan was surprised to feel suddenly angry. "I save a deer's life. The hunters were going to kill it, and my . . . my . . . *punishment* is that I can't go into the forest any more? It's not fair. What am I going to do on my own all day?"

"Don't be silly, Jeevan. There's plenty to do around here."

"There is *nothing* to do here. Nothing at all! The only reason we moved is because of you. Because you did . . . the *same thing*, Mum! Saving animals! If you hadn't freed all those rats in your old lab and got fired, we'd still be back at home."

His mum sighed. They'd been through this before.

"And now I save a deer and you're telling me I can't even . . ."

For a second or two, there was silence

as they stared at each other – Jeevan
outraged, his mum torn between concern
and exasperation.

What am I going to do all day? he
thought. *Spend my time in the lab with only
fossils for company?*

Jeevan took a deep breath and watched
his mum turn her attention back to the
microscope. He decided to let it go. Mum
would change her mind. She had to.

He let his finger trail over the neat lines
of test tubes, slides and syringes, bright
under the lab's lights. Fossils were cool but
the lab was not. Cold, yes, but cool, no.
He couldn't stay in here all day.

CHAPTER TWO

Mum took the slide out of the microscope and wheeled herself into the reactor room next to the main lab. Mum kept all the samples and specimens – the fossils – in a special fridge next to the reactor, which Jeevan was *not* allowed to touch. As far as Jeevan understood, Mum was trying to replicate the DNA from the fossils in there.

Fossils! Suddenly Jeevan remembered what he'd dug up in the bog. It was still in his pocket. Maybe if he could distract Mum with it, she'd forget about keeping him away from the forest. He followed her into the reactor room.

"Oh, Mum, I forgot – I found this in the

bog. I think it's a fossil."

Jeevan's mum stopped arranging her slides to look at what he was holding, which was when she noticed he was covered in mud.

"Oh my goodness, Jeevan! You're *filthy*! You can't come into the lab like this!"

Jeevan jumped backwards, scattering dried mud over the floor. He looked down and saw she was right. *I guess I did fall in the bog,* he thought.

CHAPTER TWO

Anjali was a great mum but she had her faults. And this was a big one: she was absolutely fanatical about keeping her lab tidy. It drove Jeevan mad. He couldn't eat a sandwich in here. He couldn't even eat an *apple* in here. *And apples don't make crumbs!* But there was no arguing with Mum on this topic. THE LAB MUST STAY CLEAN.

"Oh. Sorry, Mum."

"Just let me see the fossil," she replied grumpily.

Jeevan handed it over. "Probably a dinosaur fossil," he said.

"Probably just a deer bone," said Mum.

She pulled on some white gloves
and used a small knife to transfer the
fossil specimen onto a slide under the
microscope.

Jeevan knew that when Mum was
immersed in her work there was no point
trying to make conversation, so he settled
into a chair in the corner and switched on
the TV.

"—an eighteenth-century pocket watch
with brass detailing . . ." *Nope.* Jeevan
changed the channel.

"—so let's say a nice big 'hello' to Mr
Cuddles and Super Sock!" Next channel.

"—called Paradise Falls, a luxury hunting

lodge surrounded by nature. We spoke with Barron Fox, CEO of Fox & Co., to discuss his latest venture . . ."

Jeevan was about to change the channel again when his mum's voice rang out. "Oh, not that Barron Fox again."

"Who?" asked Jeevan, finger hovering over the remote.

His mum poked her head up from the microscope, looking at the TV. "He's this horrible businessman, always on the news – I can't stand him. He cares so little about the environment."

On screen, a short man with an awful toupée was speaking to a reporter.

"That's right. Fox & Co. will be buying an entire forest to create the *ultimate* hunting experience."

"And what about animal rights?" asked the reporter.

"Numerous activist groups are campaigning against your Paradise Falls venture."

Barron Fox gave a fake laugh. "It is human nature to hunt." He shrugged, a brown fur coat flapping on his shoulders.

Hunting. Jeevan remembered the two people in the forest. They'd mentioned a name, hadn't they?

"Mum," Jeevan said, turning quickly to face her. "The two hunters in the forest. Just before the deer thing, they were talking about a Mr Fox."

Jeevan's mum's eyes flicked from the TV to his, and they shared a worried look. "Probably just a coincidence," Anjali said, heading back to the reactor room.

Jeevan flicked channels until he found a documentary about dinosaurs.

"It may surprise viewers to learn that dinosaurs *do* still walk among us. Birds are, in fact, direct descendants of meat-eating theropods. Tyrannosaurus rex is the most famous of the theropods, although birds have evolved from smaller species . . ."

He played a game on his phone, zoning in and out of the documentary.

" —it's called imprinting. When a baby bird hatches, it forms an immediate attachment to the first thing it sees – in most cases, the mother . . ."

Mum switched off the TV. "Time to tidy up. I'm just going to type up my notes and then we'll go home."

Jeevan started in the main lab, lining up test tubes and loading the dirty slides and

CHAPTER TWO

syringes into the dishwasher. He spotted his drone that Mum had confiscated a few days ago because he was flying it indoors. *Maybe Mum will let me have that back now.*

Back in the reactor room, Jeevan's eyes landed on the row of jars containing the small stone-coloured fossils from the bog: a mammoth fossil, a sabre-tooth tiger fossil, the fossilised remains of a dodo, a megalodon shark and what his mum thought was an ancient Neanderthal toe bone. Mum spent her time analysing the DNA from these fossils, hoping it could help the endangered species of today.

T-REX TERROR

There were three test tubes on the counter. Jeevan knew they contained DNA that Mum had been analysing today. He carefully placed them into the special metal box that was supposed to go in the fridge. *Definitely no snacks in that fridge*, thought Jeevan, his stomach giving a little growl of

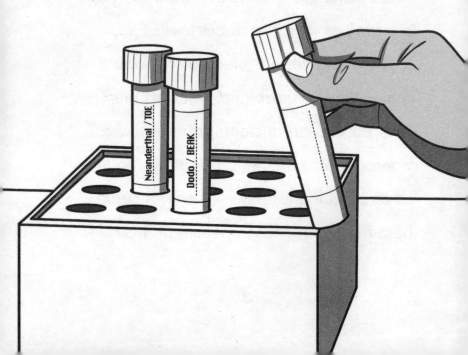

hunger. Two of the test tubes were labelled: "Dodo / BEAK" and "Neanderthal / TOE". The third one was blank. It contained what his mum had extracted from his own fossil today. Jeevan placed it carefully next to the others in the box.

He was about to take the box to the fridge when he spotted his fossil lying at the edge of the counter.

"My guess is it's a piece of a T-Rex skull, Mum," said Jeevan, picking it up and placing it in a small jar next to the mammoth tusk.

Mum didn't hear him – she'd gone into the office, a smaller room off the main lab, to type up her notes on the computer.

"Bye, Skull," said Jeevan quietly.

He backed out of the reactor room and was just shutting the door when he heard his mum call, "Don't forget the lights!"

Jeevan flicked a switch and shut the door.

3

The next morning, Jeevan and his mum headed back to the lab. Jeevan pushed the heavy doors open and stopped dead in his tracks. *Uh-oh.*

The lab was *wrecked*. Absolutely destroyed. Smashed glass everywhere, broken counters, metal stools crumpled against the walls, torn paper scattered across the floor.

Jeevan took a step inside but his shoe crunched on a broken test tube.

"Oh. My. Goodness," breathed Anjali beside him.

"There must have been a break-in," said Jeevan in a low voice.

"Who could have *done* this?" whispered his mum, running her hands over her face.

Jeevan went inside, clearing the broken glass so it wouldn't puncture the wheels on his mum's wheelchair. He couldn't believe the mess. It was the total opposite of how his mum liked the lab. TIDY. He started to look for the broom but got distracted when he saw giant cracks on

the walls and ceiling.

What had happened?

Just then Jeevan felt something knock into his leg. With a jolt of fear, he leapt back and looked down at the strangest bird he'd ever seen. It was plump and hunched, with a bald head, bright-blue feathers and a rounded beak. It bumped into his leg again and again.

"Stop it!" Jeevan called, and the bird looked up at his face with small black eyes.

"Doo-doo," it squawked.

"What?"

"Doo-doo."

Jeevan stared at this strange bird and

gave a high-pitched and very, very loud shriek. *"Aaaaarghhh!"*

The bird was a dodo! An extinct, yet somehow very- much-alive, dodo.

Jeevan stumbled around the office, heart pounding, brain malfunctioning, mouth opening and shutting. His mum arrived in the office.

"I'm okay, I'm okay!" Jeevan said. But he wasn't okay.

Anjali stared at the dodo. It stared back. And then it walked into Jeevan's leg again.

"Jeevan . . .?"

He had never heard his mum sound so uncertain before.

"I know, Mum. It's – it looks like a dodo, right?"

Anjali couldn't even respond.

But the dodo did. *"Doo-doo,"* it cooed, staring happily at Jeevan.

CHAPTER THREE

Anjali turned on the computer. "The CCTV files from last night should show us what happened."

Jeevan stood behind her, eyes on the screen, shaking his leg to ward off the over-friendly dodo.

"Doo-doo."

"Ssshh!"

"Okay, here it is," said Anjali.

Four video feeds played on the computer screen: one of the lab's exterior, one of the main lab, one of the office and one of the reactor room. The timestamp on all of them read 17.48, when Jeevan and his mum were just about to leave last night.

Jeevan saw himself in the reactor room, backing out of the door, reaching for the light switch.

Watching himself, Jeevan realised two terrible things at once: first, he had forgotten to put the box of DNA samples into the fridge; and second, that wasn't the light switch he was reaching for – it was the reactor switch!

With mounting horror, he watched himself shut the door and leave the room. A few minutes passed and nothing happened, but then the reactor in the corner started to judder. It wasn't meant to be left on for more than a few minutes at a time. Sparks began to fly from it, dissipating in the air at first, but then reaching further and further – hitting the counter, the fridge – until . . . one of them connected with the metal box on the counter.

When the spark hit the box, a bolt of electricity appeared, stretching between the reactor and the box. Static buzzed, making the video footage jump and blur. And then, when it became clear again, the metal box was fizzing, jumping and then – BANG! – it exploded.

"No . . ." said Jeevan's mum.

Jeevan couldn't manage a single word

because what came next was even worse.

In the chaos of the explosion, the room shuddering with static electricity, something was growing – yes, growing – from the metal box. At first, it looked like a small abstract blur, but then it was an animal-shaped thing, growing fast, as if someone was pressing fast-forward. Before Jeevan could even manage another shriek, a pair of wings burst out from the shape. It was a bird – the dodo! She flapped helplessly and ran into a wall. But there was more. The box continued to spark and fizz, and another

shape emerged from the explosion,
bigger, with arms and legs. *Was it a
human?* Wait, if it was coming from the
DNA, it might be . . . a Neanderthal!
Jeevan didn't have time to let that sink in
because there was another, louder boom!
The whole room shook: a giant, ferocious
T-REX erupted from the chaos and let out

a terrifying roar. Its powerful tail swished, wrecking everything on the wall behind it.

A T-Rex? thought Jeevan. *We didn't have any T-Rex DNA.*

Unless . . .

"It's Skull!" yelled Jeevan.

His mum looked at him, confused. "Skull?"

"The fossil I found! It really was a T-Rex fossil!"

Anjali covered her mouth with her hands.

On screen, the Neanderthal hid under a table while Skull snapped and roared and stomped around the much-too-small room. His giant tail knocked a giant crack in the wall and, giving one last roar, he charged through it and ran out into the forest.

Jeevan and his mum sat in silence for a very long time, interrupted by the occasional "*doo-doo*". They fast-forwarded the rest of the CCTV footage. It wasn't a break-in – it was a break-out.

Eventually, Anjali spoke. "What are we – there's a T-Rex . . . out there . . . just . . . wandering around. What do we—"

But Jeevan's mind was focused on the positives in this situation. *Dinosaurs.* "Mum, this is the greatest scientific discovery of all time! Do you realise what you've *done*?" It's amazing! Revolutionary!"

T-REX TERROR

Anjali shook her head. "But a Tyrannosaurus rex, it's so dangerous. What if he finds someone?"

What if someone finds him? thought Jeevan, remembering the hunters and their long rifles.

Taking a deep breath, Mum picked up the phone and called the police.

"Yes, I know. I know what I'm saying," Anjali's voice echoed across the lab. "I know it sounds ridiculous, officer, but I am a scientist. I have been working on a DNA study of extinct animals . . . Yes, like I told you – there is a real T-Rex in the forest. Yes, *real*. Please stop laughing, officer, this is not a joke. What? . . . Hello? *Hello?"*

She put the phone down, distraught. "They hung up on me," she said. "They told me it was an offence to waste police time. Oh, Jeevan, what on earth are we going to do?"

Jeevan had no idea. His eyes swept over the destroyed lab, the crushed metal and the shattered glass, the freaky but kind-of-cute dodo following him everywhere he went, and the enormous dinosaur-shaped hole that led from the reactor room into the forest. Where did the Neanderthal go?

Just as he was about to speak, the

doorbell rang. The dodo let out a shriek. (It sounded a lot like Jeevan's earlier shriek.) Jeevan looked at his mum. She looked at him. Her face was lined with worry. It didn't help that the dodo continued to skitter around the room. Jeevan and his mum tried to stay quiet, hoping that the person outside would go away. But then there was a knock at the door.

Ding-dong! went the doorbell again.

Uh-oh. Someone really wanted to get in.

4

D*ing-dong!*
   "Doo-doo."

Thunk.

Ding-dong!

"Doo-doo."

Thunk.

Every time the doorbell rang, the dodo
ran into the wall. Whoever was outside
was now knocking furiously.

Jeevan looked through the peephole. All he could see was an enormous white beard. There must have been a face behind the beard somewhere, though, because a voice called out. "Everything okay in there? Hello? Helloo-o?"

Jeevan and Mum stared at each other in alarm. The bearded guy was clearly not going away.

A very loud *thunk* snapped Mum into action.

"Quick," she hissed, wheeling herself across the lab. "Grab that bird and get in the reactor room. I'll deal with whoever's at the door. Just keep quiet and, whatever you do, *do not* go into the forest."

As if I want to, thought Jeevan. *There's an actual T-Rex out there.*

"Come on," Jeevan whispered, picking up the dodo, who pecked at his arms.

"Oww, I'm not food!" Jeevan yelped. "Stop it! Stop it . . . Dodo!"

Dodo did not stop it.

Jeevan had always thought it was a myth that

dodos were stupid, but this one was doing nothing to buck the stereotype. "Stop it!" Jeevan said as he bustled the dodo into the reactor room and shut the door.

Whoah. Giant wall hole. Crazy ceiling cracks. Dust floating through the air. TV ad . . . for a fizzy drink?

Jeevan was confused by the sound of a catchy advertising jingle. It was totally at odds with the *utter destruction* he was looking at. He turned towards the TV in the corner.

Someone was watching it.

Someone sitting right up close to the screen.

CHAPTER FOUR

It was the Neanderthal – there was no mistaking it. She looked about the same age as him.

No way.

Jeevan pictured the toe fossil in its little glass jar. He couldn't believe it had turned into a real, live Neanderthal.

The Neanderthal noticed Jeevan and slowly backed away from him into the corner. Her eyes widened with fear, and she held up the small knife Anjali used when dissecting the specimens.

Jeevan tried to put his hands up to reassure her, which wasn't easy to do when carrying a dodo. "It's okay," he said

as calmly as he could manage – although it wasn't too calm; he'd never been face-to-face with a knife-wielding Neanderthal before. "I'm not going to hurt you. I'm a friend. Jeevan."

The girl didn't lower the knife. Evidently, she did not feel the same way.

CHAPTER FOUR

"Jeevan," he tried again, pointing to himself. "What's your name?"

No response.

He pointed to her. "You. Name?"

She shook her head.

He wondered what some popular Neanderthal names might have been, but his mind was blank. The only thing he could think of was the label her fossil had been given. It was utterly ridiculous.

"I'm going to call you . . . Toe . . . okay?"

Just then, the next advert came on TV – for a burger restaurant. Jeevan couldn't get over the strangeness of the moment.

He was holding a dodo and watching TV with a Neanderthal. And then something even stranger happened.

Toe spoke.

"Joo-seee-end-ear-ezz-eest-abble."

"What?" said Jeevan.

Toe pointed to the TV. *"Flay-mmm-grillll-too-purr-fec-shunnn."*

Flame-grilled to perfection?

Toe was pointing urgently to the TV. *"Joo-seee! Ear-ezz-eest-abble!"*

Jeevan looked from Toe to the burger on the screen. Then back to Toe. Then back to the burger. "Juicy and irresistible?"

Toe nodded vigorously.

CHAPTER FOUR

He had to laugh. Yes, this was incredibly strange. He was standing in front of a Neanderthal who had grown from the fossil of a toe bone. And she was talking. *Talking!* She must have been watching TV all night. Clearly, she was a quick learner. And clearly . . . she was hungry.

"Are you hungry?" he asked.

Toe cocked her head. "Hun-gree," she echoed. "Veh-reee hun-gree."

"Maybe that's because you've been dead for 50,000 years," said Jeevan, although he immediately realised it wasn't a very helpful response.

"*Doo-doo,*" said Dodo, even less helpfully.

Toe looked confused and Jeevan felt
suddenly sorry for her. She must have
no idea what was going on. He walked
slowly towards her, setting Dodo down
on the floor. Toe stayed in the corner but
lowered the knife.

"Look," said Jeevan, taking out his phone
and showing her the date. "It's the twenty-
first century."

Toe squinted at the phone in Jeevan's
hand. She reached out to touch it, but as
the screen grew bright, she snatched her
hand away. "Flame!"

Jeevan and Dodo stared.

He tried his best to explain what a phone

was, but it seemed Toe's vocabulary was pretty much limited to words about burgers and fizzy drinks.

"Look," said Jeevan. We live in the present – I mean, the future – I mean, it's like the future for you, but for me it's just . . ." He trailed off, looking to Dodo for support, but even she was shaking her head.

Ok, let's try this again, he thought.

He pointed to himself. "Jeevan." He waved his arms around to indicate the modern world. "Twenty-first century."

Toe looked baffled, but amused.

Jeevan ran to the light switch.

"Electricity." He flicked it on and off. He pulled at his hoodie and jeans. "Clothes. *Fashion.*"

Toe wrinkled her nose. *"Fah-shun."* She shook her head.

He pointed at Toe. He mimed using a bow and arrow. Then he pretended to  be a lion. "Meat." He tried to mime a bonfire on the ground in front of him, but this was trickier than he'd thought. "Fire." When he looked up, he saw Toe quickly stifle a grin.

Is she laughing at me? he thought.

"We don't hunt for food any more," he said, waving his finger in a "no" motion. Toe waved her finger along with him.

"We buy food from the supermarket," Jeevan continued, trying to mime handing over money and carrying a shopping bag, but he stopped pretty quickly – he wasn't going to win a charades tournament any time soon.

"No caves," he said. "We live in houses." He made his hands into the shape of a pitched roof. Toe stared at his raised hands.

"Kids go to school."

"Skooooool."

"And we watch TV."

When Jeevan gestured to the TV, Toe started nodding enthusiastically. "Teevee!" she said, pointing happily.

Jeevan had to laugh. Toe was from the Stone Age but she already loved TV.

An advert for another fast-food restaurant came on. Toe's eyes went wide. She rubbed her stomach. "Meat. Joo-see."

Jeevan turned to Toe and pointed to himself. "Jeevan. Vegan."

He could see Toe moving her mouth to try sounding out the new words.

CHAPTER FOUR

"Jee-gunn?"

"No, I'm Jeevan. *Jeevan*. And I'm vegan. No meat." He pointed to the barbecued steak sandwich on the screen – flame-grilled – and then shook his head. "No meat."

Toe looked confused. "No meeeet?"

Jeevan shook his head again. "No meat."

"Hun-gree."

And suddenly Jeevan knew exactly how to convince Toe that he was her friend.

Food.

He backed towards the door, holding up a hand. "Wait here," he said. "Just wait right here and put the knife down. I'll get you some food."

He cracked open the door to the lab. He could hear Mum talking to Beard Guy. Jeevan crept along the wall between the reactor room and the office, doubled over to keep out of sight. He made out snatches of conversation between Mum and the visitor.

". . . possible to reverse-engineer the samples . . ." The visitor's voice was low and scratchy.

". . . the DNA was less stable than . . ." Mum sounded a bit more in control now that she was talking about science.

CHAPTER FOUR

Jeevan reached the office. He scurried around, searching for Mum's secret stash of chocolate bars – and there they were, buried at the back of a drawer. Even Dr Anjali "KEEP THE LAB TIDY" Kaur, PhD, biochemist extraordinaire and neat-freak *par excellence*, liked a cheeky chocolate bar now and then.

Jeevan grabbed one and carefully sneaked back to the reactor room.

T-REX TERROR

Toe is going to love this, he thought with a grin – but what he saw when he entered the reactor room turned his smile upside down.

Toe was holding her knife again, and she was running around the room. Her eyes were wild and excited, alert and . . . murderous.

She was chasing Dodo.

The dodo was flapping all over the place, clearly aware enough to know when it was being hunted for dinner.

"Doo-doo!"

"Nooo!" cried Jeevan, forgetting they had to keep quiet. He ran towards Toe and

Dodo, waving his arms to explain that this
bird wasn't for eating.

Toe almost crashed into Jeevan, but he
caught her. She poked her head round his
body, staring wistfully after the escaping
bird. Jeevan held Toe back, trying to keep

his face away from the pointy end of the small knife.

When he finally swung round to see where Dodo had gone, he saw the last of her tail feathers swishing through the hole in the wall.

"No, Dodo!" Jeevan yelled, letting go of Toe and running to the hole. The dodo had disappeared into the forest.

Toe raised the knife again and side-stepped Jeevan before he could do anything to stop her. She ran full-pelt through the hole, shouting as she went, "*Ear-ezz-eest-abble . . .*"

Jeevan watched Toe crash through a

CHAPTER FOUR

dense clump of bushes with a sinking feeling in his chest. Mum had explicitly told him *not* to go into the forest. He hesitated for a moment – and then off he ran.

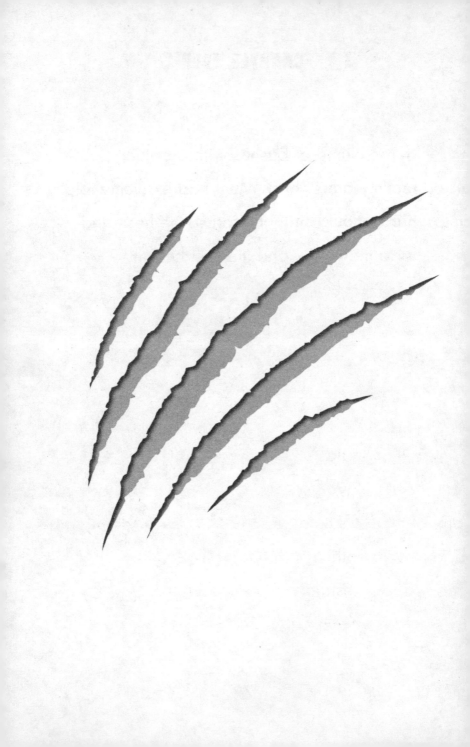

5

"Toe!" Jeevan called. "Wait!"

He caught up with her, but there was no sign of Dodo. "Let's go back," he said anxiously, gesturing towards the lab. "Dodo's gone. Bird gone."

Toe crouched down, staring intently at the ground. She looked up at Jeevan and pointed. "Find," she said.

Jeevan took a closer look. *Was there*

something in the mud? Toe was busy prodding the soil with her finger. Jeevan could see something that *could* be dodo tracks. Or it could just as easily be a hedgehog footprint. He shrugged at Toe. "We'll never find her."

Toe looked up at Jeevan in astonishment. "Find!" she said, and pointed again, as if it were the most obvious thing in the world. "Tracks!"

Jeevan shook his head cluelessly.

"Even baby can track bird," Toe said, snorting.

She's making fun of me, Jeevan realised.

"Are you baby?" said Toe with a grin

that was slowly widening.

Jeevan knew he was being insulted but he couldn't help but smile. He shook his head again.

"You don't have knife?" Toe asked.

When Jeevan shook his head a third time, she burst into laughter. "Even baby have knife!" she squealed.

It's not that *funny,* thought Jeevan.

"Let's find Dodo," he said, before adding sternly, "but no eating her!"

Toe led the way through the forest, pausing every so often to take a closer look at the ground or to touch one of the bushes they passed. Jeevan couldn't help but be impressed when Toe pointed out a snapped branch that told them Dodo had crashed through this way, or a tiny piece of grey feather, half buried in the soil, that told them Dodo had turned left here, not right.

As they made their slow progress through a knot of dense trees, Jeevan put his hands in his pockets and realised he'd forgotten to give Toe the chocolate he'd taken from his mum's office.

He unwrapped the bar and passed it to Toe, miming eating to make sure she understood what it was. She stuffed it into her mouth, chewing furiously. But then her face crinkled up and she spat out an enormous blob of chocolate on to the ground.

"Ugh!" she croaked, clutching her throat as if she'd been poisoned.

"Don't you like it?" Jeevan stared. "It's chocolate."

"Bleuuuurgh!" she said, running over to a large pond and trying

to wash her mouth out with water. Jeevan laughed. Then they both heard a familiar sound. *"Doo-doo."*

Dodo was at the other side of the pond, staring into the water.

"Doo-doo," she cooed to her own reflection.

She thinks she's made a friend, thought Jeevan, and he started towards her. Toe was right beside him.

Jeevan was about to call out when he heard a buzzing sound. It was faint, but getting louder. Before he could work out what it was, he heard a much closer whooshing sound. A large net fell on to the dodo.

Jeevan pulled Toe
down into the long
grass at the edge
of the pond and
they watched
as two figures
stepped out from behind
the trees.

One tall, one short; a woman and a
man, rifles slung across their backs. Jeevan
recognised them instantly. The hunters!

Dodo thrashed in the net, squawking for
all she was worth. Jeevan could hear the
hunters' voices clearly across the pond.

"It's a bird!" said the man.

"I can see that!" snapped the woman. "What kind of bird, though? It doesn't look like a pheasant . . . does it?"

"Well, it's definitely not a pigeon," the man replied, although he didn't sound too certain.

The two of them struggled with Dodo, who was being most uncooperative. Eventually they lifted her up in the net and started carrying her away from the pond. Jeevan spotted a green Jeep parked amongst the trees with the Fox & Co. logo on it. Before he could think of a plan, something happened that made him jump

CHAPTER FIVE

out of his skin.

His phone started ringing.

Toe turned to him, confused, while he rummaged in his pockets and pulled it out: it was Mum.

Jeevan quickly hung up and turned the phone to silent, but the damage was done. The hunters were looking around for the source of the noise. That gave Jeevan an idea. It was crazy but might just work. "Doo-doo!" he called out, as loud as he could. Peering round the thick trunk, he saw the hunters snap their heads in his direction.

He sneaked away and hid behind

another tree. "Doo-doo!"

"There's another one!" said the woman.

Toe understood his plan and creeped around the pond. "Doo-dooo!" she shouted.

The hunters jumped and looked at each other. "There's loads of them," said the man.

Jeevan and Toe moved from tree to tree, making dodo sounds. After about a minute, Jeevan was relieved to see the hunters set down Dodo's net, grab their rifles and wander off to search for the other birds.

Toe, who was closer, raced over to

CHAPTER FIVE

Dodo and cut the net with her knife. From his tree, Jeevan watched as she picked up the dodo. Unfortunately, this made the bird panic even more. She let out a massive *"DOO-DOO!"* and Toe gave a loud yelp of surprise.

The hunters must have heard, because they returned, rifles raised.

But by the time they arrived, the bird and the net were gone.

Jeevan tried to silence a laugh at the scene in front of him. The two hunters were looking very cross and confused, while a young Neanderthal holding a flapping dodo crouched calmly in the

branches above their heads. Somehow,
Toe had climbed a tree while holding
Dodo and the net. Jeevan watched in
astonishment as Toe raised one finger to
her lips in a *shhh* sign and gave Jeevan a
mischievous wink.

In one fluid motion, Toe dropped the

CHAPTER FIVE

net onto the hunters and jumped out of the tree. She raced towards Jeevan and together they ran away from the pond, hearing the hunters bickering behind them.

"Ouch!"

"Get off!"

The children ran until Jeevan spotted something familiar in the distance – it was his bike! *Yes!*

Jeevan ran towards it, but realised Toe was no longer beside him.

"Can't keep up?" he joked. Then he turned back to see where she was – and he stopped laughing right away. Toe was standing in a *gigantic* footprint.

T-REX TERROR

She looked at Jeevan, but he didn't return her gaze. He was distracted by something much *bigger* behind her.

Something emerging from the forest like a monster from a nightmare.

The T-Rex.

"Skull," whispered Jeevan.

He was absolutely enormous – a greyish-green giant, snapping tree trunks and dislodging branches as he approached. His mouth was open and he was shaking his head from side to side, showing off razor-sharp teeth. With each step, Jeevan felt the ground rumble.

"Don't move," he whispered to Toe,

who hadn't spotted the T-Rex yet. Jeevan repeated her *shhh* gesture from earlier.

But it didn't work. Toe *did* move and she *didn't* shush.

Instead, she looked around, saw the T-Rex and screamed.

Skull opened his enormous jaws in a carnivorous grin . . . and then he charged.

6

Toe ran towards Jeevan, her face a mask of terror. Jeevan leaped on to his bike, gesturing wildly for Toe to climb on the pegs by the back wheel. She jumped on, still holding the madly thrashing Dodo in one arm, looping her other arm around Jeevan.

"Go!" she cried, her voice drowned out by a huge T-Rex roar.

T-REX TERROR

She didn't have to tell him twice. Jeevan pushed off and cycled as fast as he could.

All my practice at the skate park is about to come in handy, he told himself.

They sped deep into the forest, Jeevan pedalling madly, Toe holding on for dear life, Dodo squawking and Skull in hot, hungry pursuit.

Jeevan dared a look behind him, then wished he hadn't. A glob of T-Rex spit landed on his cheek.

Jeevan wove through the tree trunks and tried to bunny hop over roots poking up from the ground, but every so often he didn't spot them in time and the bike jolted

CHAPTER SIX

violently into the air.

Skull had no such problems. The
dinosaur barrelled through the forest,
crashing through trees and bushes –
leaving pure destruction in his wake.

Jeevan veered and swerved, careful
to keep the BMX balanced, but his heart
dropped when he saw a huge fallen oak
blocking the path ahead of them. Toe let
out a screech, while Jeevan prepared
himself for a BMX stunt he'd never been
able to get right before – a 180.

He sped up and just before the bike
smashed into the tree, he boosted the front
wheels into the air, urging the back wheels

up after, and turned the bike to the left in one swift move.

Yes!

A perfect 180, and now they were headed away from the fallen oak.

T-REX TERROR

Just then Toe stiffened. Jeevan knew why immediately; he could hear it too. A growl. Not the angry growl of the T-Rex, who was still right behind them, but a lower, softer growl. It was more . . . mechanical?

He looked over his shoulder and gasped. "Hunters!"

The hunters had joined the chase in their green Jeep. They weren't after the dodo, or even trying to save the children. The woman was leaning out of the Jeep's passenger window brandishing her rifle; they were on a T-Rex hunt.

Jeevan steered his bike down a slope, which turned into a steep drop. They soared downhill. Jeevan was going faster than he'd ever cycled in his life, zooming past the trees and widening the gap between them and the T-Rex.

As they hurtled down, Jeevan's stomach sank. In a matter of seconds, they'd hit the stream at the bottom of the slope. Speeding up, he jerked hard on the handlebars. They soared into the air and cleared the stream. Landing on the other bank, Jeevan pushed off and pedalled hard, followed by the T-Rex. But there was a problem; now they were going uphill.

Jeevan's heart was pounding. His head was buzzing with fear – and the T-Rex's

deafening roars
right behind them
didn't help. Skull
was close. Too
close. Bad breath
close. Jeevan
winced at the
stink, but there
was nothing he
could do about
that, except—

"Faster!" Toe yelled.

It was getting harder to pedal the higher
they went. A strange buzzing noise made
Jeevan look around wildly. He'd heard it

before. It wasn't the hunters' jeep, which
had just managed to cross the stream.
Jeevan ignored the sound, focusing on
pedalling fast. He huffed and puffed as the

bike skidded on the steep, rocky path. And just when he thought his legs could pedal no further, the slope levelled out. Jeevan sped up. The problem was that the T-Rex and Jeep were getting faster too.

Toe pinched his shoulder and pointed. Jeevan jerked his head up and saw that a hundred metres ahead of them the path ended, cut off by a sharp, sheer drop.

A cliff edge.

The crack of a gunshot rang out. A bullet whistled past his ear. The hunters were close. But the T-Rex was closer! Skull's jaws gnashed at their back wheel, almost knocking them off balance.

CHAPTER SIX

Jeevan kept pedalling, the ground
shaking with Skull's thundering strides.
There was no turning back. There were
three choices: crash, get shot or get eaten.

"Go!" shouted Toe.

Without thinking, Jeevan accelerated up
to the edge of the cliff . . . and jumped!

7

ne moment, he was cycling fast
on the path and the next, he was
pedalling through thin air. For a second,
it felt like they were flying. Then they were
falling . . .

The bike dropped out from under them
and Jeevan and Toe tumbled through the
air. Dodo tried to flap her wings, and Toe
caught her as they plummeted. Jeevan

looked up and saw, almost in slow motion, Skull falling after them. His deep roar was accompanied by the screech of the hunters' Jeep braking sharply at the top of the cliff.

I'm going to die, thought Jeevan.

But instead of hitting the ground with a splat, a tall tree below broke his fall. He landed in a tangle of leaves and twigs with a crash. The tree shook as Skull landed heavily below. Jeevan heard a groan and looked up. Toe was hanging from a branch above. A faint "doo-doo" sound coming from the leaves confirmed that Dodo was safe too. Jeevan carefully picked out a few splinters from his hands. *Ouch.* He was covered in cuts and scratches. But all things considered, he was okay. They had all survived.

Jeevan mustered enough energy to climb up to Toe. From this high up, he could see the cliff face they'd just fallen off. It ran all the way around a giant valley in what was almost a perfect circle. In the centre of the valley was a sparkling blue lake, surrounded by dense, lush greenery. Jeevan couldn't believe this hidden place was so close to the forest. It wasn't on any of the maps Mum had shown him and he hadn't seen it when flying his drone. After the roaring, crashing, blood-thumping bicycle chase, the silence of this valley was immense.

Far below, on the ground, he saw Skull limping off into the forest. Jeevan allowed himself a sigh of relief. He couldn't believe they were actually still alive. Then Toe gave him a fright by letting out a deep, throaty victory shout.

"Aiiiieeeeeee!"

Birds fluttered out of the nearby trees.

"Come on, Toe," Jeevan said, his voice shaky. "Let's go home."

"Home. Dee-lish-uss snack?" said Toe hopefully.

Jeevan laughed. "Yes," he said. "A

delicious snack. I promise."

They picked their way down through
the branches. Toe was a lot quicker than
Jeevan, even though she was carrying
Dodo.

Jeevan, who had fallen, scraped and
bumped his way down, spotted his bike
on the ground. Its tyres were burst, the
chain had broken and the handlebar had
been bent out of shape. There was no way
they could ride it home. Not that Jeevan
knew a way out of this strange valley. He
bent down to see if he could fix any of
it, concentrating hard, when a shadow
loomed over him and the bike.

Jeevan turned and saw a tall, broad-shouldered man with an enormous grizzly beard. The beard covered more than half of the man's face. It was the man who had come to the lab earlier.

Behind the beard, it was hard to see the man's expression. His grey eyes were alert and focused, and Jeevan got the impression that this was a man who couldn't be outwitted. The children backed up towards the tree behind them, and Jeevan saw, out of the corner of his eye, that Toe had raised her knife again.

"I'm surprised to see the two of you alive," said the man in a gruff voice. Jeevan didn't know what to say. It wasn't exactly a normal way to say hello.

The man took a step forward. "I'm Griff," he said, extending a very large hand in Jeevan's direction.

"I'm not going to hurt you," he added when Jeevan didn't move.

After a few moments, Jeevan found his voice again. In his head, he could hear his mother's words: *Manners, Jeevan – where are your manners!*

"I'm Jeevan," he replied in a throaty half-croak, half-whisper.

The beard twitched sideways, and Jeevan realised the man was smiling.

"I know," said Griff, and he started sprinkling small black seeds on to the ground around him. Dodo hopped out from behind the tree and started pecking away happily.

"*How* do you know?" Jeevan said, turning back to Griff.

"Well, this is my valley," Griff said, waving his arm around, "and I know everything that goes on around here.

T-REX TERROR

I came by the lab earlier to see what was going on, because last night was . . ." Griff trailed off, as if he didn't know how to describe it.

Jeevan's heart skipped a beat. Did Griff know about the T-Rex? *How could he know?*

Then Griff continued, ". . . a very strange night indeed."

Jeevan couldn't think of anything to say.

Griff gave a small chuckle. "Don't worry, Jeevan. I know what happened at the lab last night. I saw the video footage."

Jeevan's mouth hung open.

"I own the lab," Griff explained.

Jeevan shut his mouth with a snap. Now

he was really confused. "You . . . you *own* the lab?"

Griff smiled again. His grey eyes actually twinkled. "Yes, I own it. I hired your mother to lead the research. But I never expected her to make so much progress this quickly." Griff cocked his head to one side and shuffled his feet. "I keep to myself. I don't really like being out in public," he said.

Toe stood up again and carefully slid the knife into a pocket on her side. Jeevan wanted to ask a hundred questions, but Griff turned his head to the forest, the way the T-Rex had wandered off.

"He's injured," he said, walking in that

direction and gesturing for Jeevan and Toe
to follow.

No way I'm following a T-Rex, thought
Jeevan, though he did feel a bit uneasy at
the thought of the T-Rex being hurt. It was
him who had brought the dinosaur back to
life, after all.

Toe stayed resolutely still. Dodo,
however, hopped after Griff, pecking at
seeds and *doo-doo*ing merrily.

Griff turned back to the children. "Look,"
he said, pointing to an enormous T-Rex
footprint in the soil.

Exactly, thought Jeevan. *A giant dinosaur
footprint.* If that's how Griff was trying to

convince him to follow, it wasn't going to work.

"No, look at this," said Griff, more urgently this time. Jeevan drew closer to see what Griff was pointing at and then knelt down on the ground.

T-REX TERROR

There was blood in the footprint. A lot of blood.

Jeevan felt a lump in his throat as he slowly realised what had happened.

Skull had been shot.

8

Between Griff, who knew every inch of the valley, and Toe, with her tracking skills, it wasn't hard to follow the path Skull had taken as he trampled injured through the forest. Apart from his gigantic footprints, the flattened bushes and snapped trees were a helpful giveaway.

Griff led the way through the towering pines. "This whole valley," he explained, "is off the grid. No phones, no roads – it's just me and nature."

He pointed at the cliff face that ran around the whole valley. "Thousands of years ago, this hill was actually a volcano. Where we're standing right now, this would have been the crater. After centuries of inactivity, things started to grow here, and this hidden natural sanctuary was formed."

A thought occurred to Jeevan. "How did you get here from the lab so quickly?"

"Good question. There's only one way in and out – well, apart from jumping off that cliff edge. I built a secret underground tunnel that comes out in a hidden location in the forest."

The hidden valley was definitely beautiful, but Jeevan couldn't understand why someone would go to such lengths to live alone like this.

Griff seemed to understand his confusion and began to explain. "When I was young, my family owned a huge farming company. Huge. Do you know what factory farming is?"

Jeevan shook his head.

Griff continued, "It's when the farmers do whatever they can to make the animals perfect for slaughtering – even if it's not kind to the animals. My family – well, they didn't care about the animals at all. Only about money."

Griff looked down at his hands. Clearly he was ashamed. "When I inherited the business, I closed down the farms and made sure the animals went somewhere safe. I donated money to animal charities and environmental research. I wanted to create a sanctuary for animals, and then I found this hidden valley. I took it off the grid. I wanted to get away from my old life and do something good for animals."

Griff paused as they reached another footprint, this one with much more blood in it. He looked worried as he peered into the forest, trying to work out which way to go. He spotted a trampled tree to their right and they set off towards it.

"And my mum?" Jeevan asked.

"Yes," said Griff. "Your mum. I've admired Anjali's research for a long time. I wanted to fund my own research into protecting endangered animals. So when I discovered the bog, I set up a lab to study the fossils I found. And then when I heard about the rats—"

"Rats?" Toe interrupted.

Griff laughed. "Yes, Jeevan's mother used to work in a university research facility. But she led the students in a protest where they released all the lab rats from the biology department."

Toe looked confused. Either she couldn't understand what Griff had said or she couldn't comprehend why someone would release perfectly delicious rats.

"Because rats are animals," Jeevan said passionately, looking into Toe's wide eyes. "Like you and me."

Toe mouthed, "*Me?*" and pointed at herself, looking most astonished.

"And that's why I hired Anjali," said Griff. "But I never expected that *anything* like this would happen."

CHAPTER EIGHT

Nobody needed to ask what he meant by "this" because at that moment, they found Skull.

The T-Rex was lying on his side next to three fallen trees. He was unconscious and the mud around him was slick with blood.

Jeevan wondered if they were too late. Skull didn't look good. Jeevan didn't think he'd ever seen anything so sad: a mighty T-Rex so helpless.

They slowly approached the T-Rex and Jeevan spotted a large bullet wound in his leg and two more in his side.

Jeevan carefully touched the dinosaur's leg. Skull gave a tiny growl and flicked

T-REX TERROR

his tail weakly. The T-Rex opened his eyes and stared straight at Jeevan, who jumped back in alarm. But Skull hardly reacted. Jeevan held the eye contact and saw that

Skull was an animal like any other. Like the lab rats, the deer, the hedgehog and the silly dodo Toe was cradling protectively.

Skull was an animal. And he was in pain.

Hardly realising what he was doing, Jeevan put his finger into the bullet wound on Skull's leg. Skull grunted in pain, but Jeevan quickly pulled out the bullet!

T-REX TERROR

Standing there beside the great beast, holding a blood-soaked bullet, Jeevan's eyes flicked back to Skull's. They were open and there was an awareness in them. Jeevan edged around the T-Rex's body and carefully pulled out the other two bullets. Skull was looking right at him and it was almost like the T-Rex knew what Jeevan had done for him. Then Skull shut his eyes again.

Jeevan backed away from Skull, gesturing for the others to do the same. They watched as Skull staggered up, a little unsteady. He growled weakly and started to walk away, deeper into the forest, when . . .

"*Doo-doo!*"

The T-Rex's head snapped round and Jeevan knew that his sharp eyes were focused on the three humans.

Instead of charging at them, Skull just stared. Jeevan could have sworn the dinosaur dipped his head in their direction before turning back to stomp away.

When the dinosaur was out of sight, Jeevan let out a huge sigh of relief and pulled his phone from his pocket to check

the time. Twenty-one missed calls. *Mum!*
he thought. *Oh, I am going to be in so
much trouble.*

Jeevan tried to return his mum's calls,
but he had no signal. He looked at Griff,
who shrugged and said, "Off. The. Grid.
There's no signal in the valley."

"We need to go home," Jeevan said. He
knew his mum must be so worried, what
with a T-Rex and other dangerous animals
on the loose.

Griff led the children back to the edge
of the crater. There was a giant boulder
resting against the cliff, and when Griff
pressed a button on his remote control,

it rolled aside to reveal a secret tunnel. He told them that Skull would be safe from the outside world in the valley, which had everything a T-Rex could ever want.

Jeevan grinned. "And the outside world will be safe from him too!" There was no way even a T-Rex could climb out of the crater.

Toe held up the dodo. "Dodo stay here too," she said.

Griff agreed. "She can live a happy life here. The valley is big enough for all sorts of animals to roam freely. Dodo will be fine. With all the seeds she wants."

Toe placed Dodo gently on the ground
and tried to pat her head without getting
pecked.

They said their goodbyes and Jeevan
and Toe headed into the secret tunnel. He
left his bike with Griff, who said he would
try to fix it. The tunnel was big enough for

a car to pass through, and it sloped down and down. Jeevan used his phone light to guide them. Finally, they arrived at an exit. Jeevan pressed a button on the wall of the tunnel and a large door opened. They were back in the forest!

As soon as they walked through, the doors shut behind them. The exit was completely covered in greenery – there was no way they would have ever noticed it just passing by. Looking around, Jeevan realised they had in fact already passed it when they were cycling up the hill.

"Okay," he said. "Let's go back to the lab now."

"Not so fast," came a sharp voice.

It was the hunters. They stepped out calmly from behind a big rock, smug smiles on their faces.

They looked at each other, then at the children, then at each other again. Their smiles widened. They raised their rifles.

9

Staring down the barrels of the rifles, Jeevan froze. He could sense Toe next to him, not daring to move either.

Stay calm, he told himself. *Stay calm.*

The woman took one hand off her rifle and fished a phone out of her pocket. She tapped away for a few seconds and then started talking to the screen. She was on a video call.

T-REX TERROR

Jeevan glanced at Toe. She was reaching for her knife. He shook his head.

"Mr Fox," said the woman, "I think you need an update on the situation. We are at the Paradise Falls location but we've run into some . . . er . . ."

"Spit it out, Smith!" came an angry voice from the phone. "I don't have all day. I'm supposed to be in a meeting right now."

"Yes, sir." Smith looked flustered, but she carried on. "Well, we came across an unusual bird in the forest, which we – well – we think may have been a dodo. But then some children stole the bird, so we

followed them and that's when we saw . . .
the . . . the . . ."

"The *what*?"

"The T-Rex, Mr Fox, sir. There's a T-Rex
out here in the forest! We tried to capture it,
or chase it down, but it ran so—"

Mr Fox's voice cut her off. "Are you out
of your mind?" he bellowed. Smith winced.
"I'm literally holding my pen," shouted Fox,
"about to sign the land deal – and you're
talking about dinosaurs?"

"Sir," the other hunter chimed in, poking
his head nervously into the video frame.
"Smith is telling the truth. We chased the
T-Rex through the forest. But it got away."

T-REX TERROR

"Jones, are you seriously going on about a T-Rex as well? Are you for real?"

Smith and Jones looked at each other.

"Honestly, sir," Smith said, "it was an actual T-Rex." Then her eyes lit up. She had an idea. Smith turned the phone around so it was pointing at Jeevan and Toe.

"Tell him," she said to the children, her eyes wide and eager. "Tell him about the dinosaur."

Jeevan recognised the man as Barron Fox, CEO of Fox & Co., squinting angrily out of the phone. Jeevan's mind raced. If he pretended there was no T-Rex, Smith and Jones would look completely crazy.

Which would
be hilarious. But
denying it would
also mean that
Fox would sign
the deal and buy
the land for his
hunting lodge.
Which would be
awful. Jeevan
imagined all those
hunters coming

here, crunching through the bushes and
shooting at the amazing wildlife. He took a
deep breath. "They're telling the truth," he

said, forcing himself not to sound scared. "There really is a T-Rex here!" he said. "It's best if everyone just stays away. For your own safety."

Smith turned the phone back to face her and smiled. "See?"

Fox's response was loud and clear: "Enough of this silliness," he barked. "I'm signing the deal now. Dinosaurs, honestly." And he hung up.

The grins quickly disappeared from the hunters' faces. Smith looked angry while Jones looked worried. "What are we going to do about them?" he asked, nudging his head towards Jeevan and Toe.

The children stayed still, watching the hunters argue about the pros and cons of letting them go.

"We can't just let them walk away . . ."

"What do you want to do? Take them to Mr Fox?"

"Oh, don't be ridiculous. How would it look if—"

"*DOO-DOO!*"

From nowhere, Dodo appeared, squealing and flapping her wings.

T-REX TERROR

She charged at the hunters, who were so surprised they fell over.

"*Doo-doooo!*" she screeched, flapping her feathers in their faces before running through their outstretched arms and into the woods behind them.

Smith and Jones got to their feet and started to chase the dodo. Jeevan heard the loud buzzing sound he'd noticed earlier. What was it? Just then, something small and black came whirring through the trees and Jeevan finally realised what the source of the noise was: a drone! *His* drone.

Mum!

CHAPTER NINE

Smith and Jones tried to run away from
the drone,
which was
buzzing
furiously
towards them,
when – CLUNK! – they
bashed heads and fell to the ground.
Out cold.

"Thanks, Mum!" yelled Jeevan as he
and Toe rushed past the hunters to catch
Dodo. She had stopped and was flapping
excitedly.

"Good girl, Dodo!" said Jeevan, petting
her bald head. Dodo jumped into his arms.

Jeevan pointed Dodo towards the secret tunnel. She must have followed them through it.

"It's safer for you back in the hidden valley, Dodo," he said, feeling a bit silly for trying to talk to a bird.

Toe chimed in, "Lots of big flavours in valley. Always fresh. Flame-grilled and seasoned to perfection."

Jeevan paused to look at Toe. Maybe he would get her to watch something else on TV later. Then he put the dodo on the ground and gently nudged her back towards the bushes.

The dodo jumped back into his arms.

CHAPTER NINE

He tried again, softly shoving Dodo in the direction of the tunnel, but she hopped neatly into his arms again.

Jeevan remembered the documentary he watched last night at the lab. Some birds imprint on the first thing they see. And the morning after the lab incident, Jeevan was the first person she met.

Oh no, thought Jeevan. *Dodo thinks I'm her mum!*

While he didn't think he was quite ready to be a mum, Jeevan felt a little bit flattered. He gave Dodo a squeeze and said, "Okay, let's go home. Maybe Mum will let me keep you!"

T-REX TERROR

Smith and Jones started to stir.

"Time to go!" said Jeevan.

They ran off as fast as they could.

10

Jeevan spotted his mum waiting anxiously outside the lab.

"Jeevan!" she cried, and he wrapped his arms around her in the biggest hug. The hug made Jeevan feel happy and safe, but then he remembered Toe. He peeked out at her over his mum's arm. She was watching, curious. He felt kind of embarrassed.

T-REX TERROR

"I was so worried," said Mum quietly. "The animals . . . you weren't answering your phone. I told you *not* to go into the forest! Why didn't you answer your phone? I tried to follow you with the drone but then I lost you. Where have you *been*?"

Toe answered, "Off. The. Grid."

Anjali stared. "You can speak?"

Anjali's jaw dropped and

CHAPTER TEN

she looked like she was about to start asking a *lot* of questions.

"Can we go home, Mum?" said Jeevan. "I'll tell you everything on the way."

Jeevan wheeled his bike along the path and caught Anjali up on the rather surreal day they'd had.

". . . and then we climbed down the tree and someone called Griff found us. He—"

"Yes, he introduced himself to me this morning. If only you'd just stayed in the lab! None of this would have happened. The thought of you running around with that T-Rex!" Anjali shook her head. "I'm so glad you're okay, Jeevan," she said.

"It was all Dodo's fault," Jeevan said, pointing to the dodo, who had just walked head first into a tree.

When they reached their bungalow, shaded by broad oaks and surrounded by small apple trees, Jeevan turned to his mum. "Can Toe and Dodo stay with us?"

CHAPTER TEN

"Okay," she said, after thinking it through. "But Dodo is your responsibility."

Jeevan nodded ecstatically. He'd always wanted a pet.

Anjali hadn't quite finished yet. "I'm talking feeding – and cleaning up after her."

Jeevan nodded a little less enthusiastically, but he agreed.

Anjali was making sabzi for dinner that night – Jeevan's favourite. She brought out all the ingredients from the pantry and showed Toe how to wash the vegetables.

T-REX TERROR

Jeevan laughed at how Toe's face lit up with utter delight when she saw how the tap worked. It wasn't long before the kitchen floor had turned into one big puddle.

Toe passed the vegetables to Jeevan, who diced them up carefully, trying to show Toe that he could, in fact, use a knife.

Dodo splashed happily on the floor and pecked at the table legs.

While Anjali sautéed onions and ginger, she told the children about the implications of their discovery today. "I can actually analyse the T-Rex's habits, movements, routines – even his secretions! It will provide a much more well-rounded view of dinosaur lifestyles than DNA alone . . ."

Jeevan was surprised but pleased that Mum was excited about the T-Rex, and not angry.

". . . and that could be the key to saving future species from extinction!" Anjali said brightly, adding spices into the pot.

Jeevan's mouth started to water. He hadn't eaten in . . . well . . . all day!

". . . the question is, *how* to study the T-Rex safely?" Anjali continued, more to herself than anyone else. "Sedation? Building a viewing station . . .?"

"What about with deee-licious snack?"

Toe said, and Jeevan smiled when he realised she was listening to every word his mum said.

"Interesting," said Anjali, looking more closely at Toe through clouds of steam. "But we'll need to avoid domestication if we want to study him without bias."

Toe nodded happily, although Jeevan was pretty sure she didn't know what Anjali was talking about. He certainly didn't.

Anjali added the chopped vegetables to the pot. They sizzled enticingly. She carried on talking. "In the morning, I'll alert the authorities. They'll have to listen to me

CHAPTER TEN

this time, especially when I show them the
dodo. This is the scientific breakthrough
of the age. People need to know about it.
Jeevan, think of all the things—"

But Jeevan interrupted her.

"Mum, no," he said, his voice louder
than he'd intended.

Anjali looked surprised. "Why not?"

"We can't tell other people about this,"
said Jeevan. "Not yet. Think about the two
hunters today. They shot Skull three times!
And think of all your old jobs, Mum. And
all the cruel experiments those labs did
on the animals. People won't treat Skull
kindly."

T-REX TERROR

Anjali looked proudly at Jeevan. She nodded her head and smiled. "You're right. *We* brought him to life, so *we* have to protect him."

Jeevan was relieved to hear his mum say "we". He felt an awful lot of responsibility for turning on the reactor last night.

"Now that Barron Fox has bought the whole forest," Anjali continued, "we need to be extra careful. Imagine what a whole hotel of hunters would give to catch a T-Rex or a dodo. We just can't let them."

Suddenly, Jeevan heard a low growl.

He looked around quickly, fear making his heart race.

CHAPTER TEN

But it was only Toe. Toe's stomach, to be precise. She was gazing at the simmering pot with pure longing.

Anjali smiled. "Dinner's ready," she said, and the three of them made their way to the table, bringing bowls and cutlery.

Toe ate with a relish that could not be called polite. *Manners, Toe – manners!*

"Doo-doo," said Dodo, pecking at Jeevan's leg under the table. He secretly gave her a piece of roti and grinned when she flapped her wings happily.

His mum continued to talk about how the discovery might help save endangered species from going extinct. Jeevan's imagination wandered – what if they could bring back mammoths and sabre-tooth tigers and pterodactyls? What if they could save the endangered rhinos and the elephants and the polar bears?

CHAPTER TEN

Jeevan looked down at Dodo, who was trying to eat the chair leg. His mum changed the topic and started asking Toe question after question about Stone Age hunting implements and fire-lighting techniques. Jeevan grinned – yesterday he'd been lonely and bored, today he had a brand-new friend and a pet, and they'd all helped to save a real-life T-Rex! He listened to Mum and Toe talk. Everything was calm now, but Jeevan had a feeling that today wasn't going to be his last adventure. This was just the beginning.

THE END

XTINCT!

LOOK OUT FOR MORE EXCITING ADVENTURES IN THE XTINCT! SERIES

There are more extinct animals in . . .

TIGER HUNT

The reactor room stood empty and silent. Toe shuffled her feet. Dodo was growing restless. Jeevan, Anjali and Griff held their breath.

. . .

And then something *did* happen.

Jeevan heard it before he saw it. A buzzing sound grew from a faint whine to a solid static *bzzzzzz*. The reactor juddered and shook as tiny flickers of electricity shot out from it. The flickers became larger sparks, which reached further and further into the room, eventually landing on the stainless steel workstation at its centre. Sparks flew around the room as if the lab were caught in a lightning storm. The hair on Jeevan's arms stood on edge – surely this wasn't safe! He took a deep breath and then saw one spark land on the metal case that held the DNA. The fizzing spark bloomed into a bolt of electricity that stretched between the workstation and the reactor.

The bolt fluctuated in intensity for a few seconds, growing brighter and then fading. It was mesmerising but also a bit scary. The brightness of the light hurt Jeevan's eyes but he couldn't look away. Toe took a small step back from the window. The metal case started jumping and jolting. Higher. Faster. And then . . . *BANG!* – a huge explosion shook the room with a burst of static-filled smoke. A shape began to grow out of it.

It emerged in the glowing electric light, sprouting a tail, growing fur and finally sprouting two enormous curved fangs.

"No . . ."

Gasp.

"It can't be . . ."

"But how . . . ?"

"*Doo-doo.*"

"It's a . . ."

Silence.

Then the animal roared.

"It's a sabre-tooth tiger," whispered
Jeevan.

READ XTINCT! TIGER HUNT
TO FIND OUT WHAT HAPPENS NEXT . . .

TYRANNOSAURUS REX

The T-Rex name means 'tyrant lizard king' and they were named that way because these predators were big meat eaters. Their 60 teeth could grow up to 30 cm long, and one bite from their massive jaws could create 6 tonnes of pressure!

These dinosaurs had a great sense of smell and were fairly speedy – walking as fast as 12 kph. They lived at the very end of the Late Cretaceous period, which was roughly 90 to 66 million years ago.

HEIGHT: 4 M
WEIGHT: 7,000 KG
INTELLIGENCE: 8/10
SPEED: 6/10
DANGER: 10/10!

HOMO NEANDERTHALENSIS

Neanderthals were skilled
hunters who could control
fire and even make art! They
had loud, high-pitched voices
and lived in Europe and
Asia from about 400,000 to
40,000 years ago. Evidence
from fossils shows us that

**HEIGHT: 1.6 M
WEIGHT: 78 KG
INTELLIGENCE: 10/10
SPEED: 6/10
DANGER: 7/10**

Neanderthal and modern human DNA separated
around 500,000 years ago. Believe it or not,
some of us have roughly 2% Neanderthal DNA
in our bodies!

RAPHUS CUCULLATIS

Dodos were big flightless birds that evolved in isolation on the island of Mauritius. They were descendants of pigeons. Until humans arrived on the island, they lived peacefully with no predators. They only lay one egg at a time, which sadly meant that when humans began hunting them, their population quickly dwindled. The last living dodo was seen in July 1681.

HEIGHT: 1 M
WEIGHT: 20 KG
INTELLIGENCE: 1/10
SPEED: 4/10
DANGER: 0/10!

Over 99% of all organisms that have ever lived in the world are now extinct. In many ways, extinction is part of evolution. But it's very worrying how quickly animals and plants we know and love are currently disappearing.

Human activities like hunting, overfishing and cutting down forests, and the effects of the climate crisis that humans have created, are causing mass extinction. **One million species out of eight million are now threatened with extinction.**

Right now, roughly **150 species are lost for ever every single day.** We all need to take action to slow the rate of extinction and save our animals, plants and fungi.

WHAT WE CAN DO TO HELP

While the global problem of extinction can feel much too big to solve, there are small steps we can all take to try and help.

1. Walk or cycle

The burning of fossil fuels is a huge factor in our climate crisis and the high rate of extinction. Make small changes like walking to school instead of going in a car to reduce your carbon footprint.

2. Eat less meat and dairy

Many forest have been destroyed to make space for meat and dairy farms. Cows also produce a lot of methane which is an especially bad greenhouse gas.

3. Avoid palm oil

Rainforests are being cut down to meet high demands for palm oil. It is found in products like chocolate, margarine and biscuits.

4. Use less water

Switch off the tap when you brush your teeth and shower instead of taking a bath to reduce the amount of water you use!

5. Careful what you flush!

Whatever goes down your toilet ends up in our oceans. So never flush anything plastic to help protect underwater habitats.

6. Rewild green spaces

Plant trees, shrubs and flowers if you have a garden, to provide habitats for bees, birds and other animals. But make sure not to use fertiliser or pesticides! They enter the food system and harm animals.

7. Reuse, reduce, recycle

Many extinctions are a result of how much we consume. If we use less, we have a smaller impact on the world.

www.HACHETTECHILDRENS.co.uk